# Bottle bank

# HELEN PLETTS

# Bottle bank

# Acknowledgements

Thanks to the editors of the following publications who first published some of these poems: *Aesthetica, www.ink-sweat-and-tears.com*

*Bottle bank* was longlisted for the Bridport prize in 2006

# Contents

# Broken door

Afterwards, we almost forgot how it started.

Only the blood on the glass oozed the painful moments.

Hold his arm, you said to me. I held what was left of it,
as his fist pierced the glass which sank into the flesh like crystals;
haphazard, jagged edges, that wouldn't give up the limb.

We sat down in the fragments on either sides of the door,
his spent fury and the wreckage between us, unable to free him.
All three of us hating his bully of a father,
holding onto the flesh and blood, while some silent hope about helping
was drowned out by the oncoming sirens.

# Cirkus

I can't understand the clown
but the red looks beautiful -
gold braid bitten into the fibres.

The lion tamers
(ticket collectors on Sundays)
have fallen under the gymnast's cloak
of sand dust.
I swear she kicked them as she left the ring
 - their tongues pawing at her tights.
But she is the one snarling
at the broom boys
who left grit on the star;
sharp under her toes.

Side splits in the silk
part like a ripe red mouth
and the red swallows hard.

The drip of silver and turquoise,
the strip of air
lashes over the heads
of six black Russian stallions
and the smell of horse
straw-smart and welcome,
brings the rush of animal.

A Camel dances the token Sahara waltz -
her face a tea-sipping marchioness.
Fur dewlaps a-ruffling
she bows out like the horses.

And the faith of the straight-backed boy in blue
graces a stack of white wooden chairs
(no net).

# The boats on the lake are cold

The boats on the lake are cold.
The sheen of reflection a coated mist.

The jetty wood soft dark-soaked-morning,
and I am a boat again.

The deep dancing bell sounding out now
and the shuffling man
who is always travelling past.

Always travelling past
and still on the same street.

He pauses for the breaths
the bells give to him between
their own sounds.

Their own sounds
dull with the mist now.

Dull with the steps
I left behind me.

That leave me.

That pass him.

Always passing.

And there is only one street,
snaking the lakeside.

And I must face him tomorrow
shuffling towards me
bringing that time
with him again.

# Rock concert in Ostrava

This is no-money country, where eyebrows
meet in the middle, over the brim of a
wheelchair trim, and handicap is king.

Guppy mouths touch-fit the bottle's neck;
sleek, slim vessel of forgetfulness, stem
of quietly disarrayed fertility.

Something in the sad solace of disunity;
hound-eyed, bloodshot; loop-jowl-crazy.
He danced, and was it the pills dancing ?

Sent him spiralling, frog-footed;
mute tendons tightened,
deformed, in trousers calf-height.

# The new boy

You were painting, your chair close to mine.
I found you sheltering under my pregnant form many times,
cowering, cleaning your brush in the water.
Turning the clean water murky
while holding your breath at the same time.
Finally, you asked me
with great delicacy, about your safety,
if ever you were to be alone with the other staff.
I mumbled quietly about the value of open doors
and safety in numbers
but looking into your eyes I knew
you already felt their hands on you,
on top of the marks from the last place
and the place before that.
(don't ever get too close, my boss said)
So I pressed your face against the face of my unborn.

# Travelling

You have been travelling with me for decades;
even before you were born;
your toothbrush next to mine in my suitcase,
the bristles damp from the cold water in our last hotel.

I tipped the porter through your fingers;
your napkin wiped my lower lip;
clean, white linen you had straightened
by your plate at dinner.

There was a fold, a crease in the napkin,
like the gristle-spine of a chicken carcass
springing at my touch; indelibly pressed into the fibres,
like my laundry tags with your name on.

# The cyclist's leg

That is what it reminded me of -
a closed, black umbrella.

He was cycling beside the car.
The yellow of his waistcoat
was the first thing we saw
- not the leg -
which had been removed at the knee.

The other tendon, functioning;
rippled like a bronzed stallion's haunch
working twice as hard.

The stump -
dressed with a black shiny staff
tapered into the shoe;
like a thin, polished piano-leg
flickering sunlight through stroboscopic spokes.

And I could see him dancing to music,
maybe Smetana,
waltzing with that leg,
like a real leg moves
secretly,
inside the leg of a dark trouser.

# On the other side of the sheets
*(for Sarah Hilary)*

I can't remember how I came to be
on the other side of the sheets;
him beneath me
(though he was always on top,
 always the 'General').

In a breezed manner he would
exclaim away the brittle actions
we performed together.

I'd ponder at these, later,
wiping his chin
after the chicken soup
(he never let me blow on the spoon)
but he let me blow my wet breath
into the crackle of his chest
and cover his bony hips with my thighs
his lower lip ajar, thermometer-ready,
but this time the cold glass rod
remained, tip down, in the cup.

# Narcissus

Yesterday,
the arc of sunlight on the water
appeared, halo-gold,
and framed your face with mine.
Lips, water-pressed,
I smile-lapped; kitten-meek;
with pinking tongue.
And I wondered how I might have missed

your beautiful brow curve,
your eyes; dark; ripple-dancing with my heart.
And when I fold my arms
about my form tonight,
with the white moon's fleshless jowl at my shoulder;
the still night will whisper-fill with love.

# Builders: Czech Republic – summertime

The long hot
stretches into the echo of dog.
A lathe sings. Pitch brilliant
and gilded in sunlight.

When the lathe stops
the radio winds the dog up even more,
but only the head
and stretching jaws, through the gate,
can participate.

I take out three beers
furred with cold air from the fridge,
I break off the caps
'Danke'
(They think I'm German
  when they see my blonde hair).
But they curl their lips
and show me their brown teeth
and tilt, and smile at me
through frothed gold.

I didn't invade your country
until now,
(I tell them, anyway)
and
I didn't come in a tank.

# The nightwatchman

If my body is swollen,
my mouth open,
gaping
you will know that I am no-longer listening
to the stars, the echoes of the dark.
That the spine you chose for me
is weightless, curving, letting my head loll,
letting the thieves take it all.

And the yellow jacket,
was the colour supposed to keep me awake ?
Remind me of the sun on a bright day ?
Rays at play on my forehead
forcing me to close my eyes in another way.

In the heat of this basement car park
I am buried alive
warm in a way no other fireside
could offer me this winter.
And when you find me, head tilted,
watching the dark,
I will be out on the streets again
kicking the white snow ahead of me.

# Medusa

I shade my own eyes;
when my glance returns
like an unwelcome lover's kiss,
Planted here upon my forehead
amidst the snakelet eyes; the
twisting heads. My hairdresser works
blindfolded, with bows and beads but
he is confounded by bites; his charges

are extortionate.
So, I may let myself go;
an untidy, serpenty, wrangle-headed
single. The stone-turning hardly
compensates for the cavernous,
solitary echo of slither and slithe.

# To the black papier-mâché horse in my study

All of your life you have been dark,
black, stick thin legs for support
but not structureless in thought,
enough to stand without a leaning book.

Your neck, golden-about with beads
from a Christmas tree - but they suit,
and serve as plethora of pupils to your eyeless form
a golden star belt, midnight strung

beneath your dreadlock droop of untamed mane,
that brush and bristle can not separate,
as if a fit of sweat about your neck, had broken
from the paper in a canter; twisting it, full hurricane.

The glue smell dusty dressed with ribbon saddle,
tidy to your ribs and tucked beneath.
And round your throat a neckerchief,
tied, timeless, settled by a child's hand.

Strange substances are folded in your flesh,
flour and glue that plumped the brush,
oozed over thumb and nail; dried lump hard on the hands,
to be picked at later like a crowded nose.

Your nose - more dog, than equine - fits my hand,
I hold you this way when I lift you up,
the painter's dry patch, bright beneath your chin,
like some Eastern counterbalance; white against the black.

# Zeus

It is hard, when there is
so much choice.
So much of my own design
already walks the earth;
wakes and breathes.
And one more seed
where to put it ?
Well, her nakedness

drew an unusual respect from me
and I wanted to cover her completely
with my great, white wings,
the lighter down spilling off me
into the air like confetti
and into her mouth, open wide with surprise.

# Bottle bank

A lean-trousered scrabble;
Pressed aside the green-breast-curve, toe-tipped
Arched form a-gape-reaching,
Visage-crimson-cold.
A jagged white slit creases the cheek;
And the human bright-blue-eye
Echoes love lost, the pricelessness of heart;
Scattered, like the glass shards
You hopelessly filter. Your stick twists
But it won't stretch, nor grasp without prehensile
Tendency, the bottle's neck.

# Hylas and the nymphs
*(apologies to Waterhouse)*

Maybe I could just cop a feel,
without getting my toes wet,
throwing my whole self in. I mean,
it's not as if I'm going to marry
one of them, or all of them for that matter.
But their deep brown hair, swirl-settles on the water
with the weed fronds and the lilies.
And I am hot with excitement and the sun on my back;


urging. And when they started to sing
they strung my neediness, lyre-like
and so I step in. Feel the cold now, up to my waist,
reach out to touch a soft white breast,
all the while filling with water
as another drags my legs from under me.

# Sellotape

It's up to you whether you curl up on me and
twist again;

taking so long to let me scrape my nail under your tail,
wrapping up against me

leaving the sharp adhesive scent of you on my hands
that gets stronger with every pull.

And stranger than this,
even though I try to deftly cut you up into neat strips,

you want to hold on to me;
every trace of me, becomes you

in your glistening strip, as you isolate and snatch my fingerprints,
decoding me.

# Hephaestus

The first forbidden fire-lick,
was eye-catching;
It swooped me up,
made my heart beat,
So that I pressed my face even nearer,
'til it was smutty-blackened,
'til I could wipe my greasy black finger trails
along my clothes;

trace my addiction.
Blow after blow forged the metal's form,
And if I could,
I touched my delighted,
singed-tipped-fingers to the strangely-formed,
fiery surface, before it cooled.

# Learning

Before all this,
I safely shuffled papers up and down my desk,
(rolled backwards and forwards on these little wheels)
before a fit of scruples sent me to work round the other side of the desk,
jammed up my nostrils
with the testosterone of out-of-control adolescence.

Before I stood here,
asking you if you had any more reefers
 - not to keep supplying the art class -
because you had taken over the dealing business from your uncle
at fifteen.

Later, dripping with bling, and with love bites the size of oysters,
I realised you were earning more than me.
Certainly having a good time.

How are you gonna keep track of all that money I asked
if you don't even know how to write your name ?

I was big and round with my second baby.
With a mortgage to pay for.
You were awkward and appeared after I threw stones at your window.
(pick him up on the way to work, you have a way with him,
 my boss said)
You appeared at the window, wrapped in a duvet, said you had no socks.
Let me in, I shouted, I'll find you a pair of bloody socks.

When I heard you were in prison, I sighed like a pair of bellows
that would have inflated those two socks you wore that day
into a couple of black woollen balloons.

# Icarus

Before the honeyed wax was soft
it was quill-brittle-stalked,
and rubbed, scratchily on my shoulders.
Each feathered stem
a pellucid knife-nib,
cutting me, well before
I felt myself rise and fall
in the thermal of the sun's breath,

full on; hot.
My finger tips clipped my father's eagle-blades
and tumbling together, I clawed out
each brown mottled wing shaft;
watching the ever distinctive white, speckle-fleck
of the Emperor bird, descending below me.

# And what will they say about me ?

And what will they say about me ?
When I'm lying there, not listening, as usual;
the March wind still swirling, conch-caught in my ears;
the pearl-pink paradise of soundlessness, save for the

nothing of oceans rushing through. And I have been
riding oceans; board-clinging, spirit-spent like glue,
it clings and I don't know why, and in the scheme of things
is grasping through and through.

So when the psalms begin; the ones I never chose,
the verses that they never heard me sing,
out of the mouth they never thought I'd close,
I'd like to wake and burst the box

and vent forth in my shroud, to call the boys
if they have time to spare, to come if they dare
with fiddler's bow and drum, and white-face-pasted white upon,
march the dreadful agony, outright with them.

# I am Lazarus come from the dead….

Did I start to decompose ?
My cadavery-yellow complexion;
does it scare you ?
Does it matter that I tuck flesh and bone
behind my robes
Baba Yaga style ?
Do I come out of folklore,
with translucent skin of parchment,

to speak to you of life's frail cusp;
through spittle-less lips ?
And if it were
to begin to rain right now,
would I sponge-spring to life,
or silently dissolve under the first drop ?

Printed in the United Kingdom by
Lightning Source UK Ltd., Milton Keynes
136606UK00001B/397-435/P